SHIP OF
GHOULS

book eleven of the matchmaker mysteries series

elise sax

Ship of Ghouls (Matchmaker Mysteries – Book 11) is a work of fiction. Names, characters, places, and incidents are the products of the author's imagination or are used fictitiously. Any resemblance to actual events, locales, or persons, living or dead, is entirely coincidental.

Cover design: Elizabeth Mackey
Edited by: Novel Needs
Formatted by: Jesse Kimmel-Freeman

Printed in the United States of America

elisesax.com
elisesax@gmail.com
http://elisesax.com/mailing-list.php
https://www.facebook.com/ei.sax.9
@theelisesax

For all of the Matchmaker Mysteries Readers. I'm so grateful.

ALSO BY ELISE SAX

CHAPTER 1

At some point, we all get in a rut. If your relationship is all about the same old, same old, force it onto a new path. Go on a road trip! Or better yet, go on a cruise. Cruise ships have an all-you-can-eat midnight buffet. All you can eat crab legs might not get you out of a rut, but at least you'll have a belly full of crab legs.

Lesson 2, Heart Advice from
Gladie Burger

For some reason, Spencer always made the bed. It was one of the good things about being married, and there were a lot of good things about being married, it turned out.

It had been almost two months since we said "I do" and our dream house disintegrated in a huge post-wedding pile-up. I didn't want Spencer to know it, but I was relieved that our dream house was now Pompeii, post-volcano. I loved my grandmother's house, which for me was home and the only home I'd ever known. It was true that we didn't have a refrigerator just for champagne or a giant island in the kitchen with an inlaid computer monitor, not to mention a workout room and a sauna, but my grandmother's house was a beautiful Victorian home, full of history and happy memories.

Cozy.

Spencer didn't seem to be too sad about the demise of our custom-made home, either. Occasionally when he would go to work, he would pause at his car, look wistfully across the street at the rubble of our house, and sigh. But otherwise, he seemed happy in our newlywed home.

I explained to him that we weren't going to get hit, financially. The rubble of our house would get sold, and we would turn a good profit. I was sure of it.

I had seen it.

That's right, I had the gift.

The gift didn't turn out to be an all-seeing eye. I couldn't tell when every little thing was going to happen or read minds, but I always knew when to wear a sweater or bring an umbrella. It was also helping me make matches left and right. I had turned into a dynamo matchmaker. A whiz. I could do no wrong in the love business.

For instance, I knew that Molly Evans should be with Jake Robbins. It wasn't an obvious match. She was six-foot-two and a librarian, and he was a five-foot-four boxer, but I knew that they would make each other happy, and that's what I was going to tell them at an early morning match greet I had set up.

"What're you doing?" Spencer asked pulling me back into

bed. "Where are you going?"

"Molly and Jake are coming to meet each other this morning, and I need to dress professionally."

"You mean you have to brush your teeth? Come on, we've got time."

Since we had gotten married, we had fallen into a morning routine. Spencer woke me up at the crack of dawn, and we'd jump all over each other like newlyweds until around six-thirty. Then, we would take a communal shower and possibly do some more down and dirty monkey sex while the water was still hot. After we were clean, Spencer would make the bed, and we would go downstairs and eat breakfast.

My grandmother was still on her cruise with Ruth, and it was just Spencer and me in the house, outside of matchmaking hours. It had taken a little while to get used to not having Grandma there, but not too long. At first it was like Spencer and I were playing house, that it wasn't really our home and that we were just pretending to be adults. But that ended fast.

We quickly adapted to our new roles as grownups with our own house. I got used to being the "wife," and Spencer seemed to be born to be the "husband." We had traded bedrooms with my grandmother, and we finally had enough space for Spencer's clothes. Our morning routine just sort of happened organically. Without discussion between us, we fell into a rhythm.

I had to admit that there was little in my life that gave me more joy than eating a bagel and drinking a cup of coffee with

Spencer at seven o'clock every morning. But this morning I had a lot to do, and I couldn't let Molly and Jake down. I didn't have time for our normal routine.

"Would you be upset if we skipped the morning bed noogy?" I asked Spencer.

Spencer shot me his best hurt puppy look. "No noogy? Why? Why?"

"Molly and Jake are going to be here right on time, and they're going to get right down to the match greet. Then, Jake is going to have a flat tire, and Molly's going to give him a ride. That's when they'll fall in love. So you see, I'm on a tight schedule. It has to happen on time."

Spencer arched an eyebrow. "Okay. You know, it's hard to argue with your wife when she's a witch."

"I'm not a witch. I just have the gift."

"Okay. Okay, Glinda. No bed noogy. But we'll give the shower noogy a bigger punch today. I've been meaning to try out the soap dish."

I couldn't lie. I was as intrigued as I was scared about the soap dish remark. "Deal," I said.

Spencer turned on the shower, and we walked inside. As much as possible, he was very good about letting me have the spot under the showerhead. I took in his nakedness and sucked air between my teeth. Spencer was very impressive naked. Even more impressive than he was dressed in his fancy clothes. He had washboard abs and muscles everywhere. And then there was his face, which on a scale of one to ten was a number so high that only Stephen Hawking could have counted to it.

Even without a fancy workout room at home, Spencer was diligent about exercising at the police station every day. The only exercise I got was sex with Spencer and minimal walking to get coffee. I placed my palm on his chest with my fingers splayed. "You're in such good shape. I can't compete."

Spencer wrapped his arms around me and pulled me in close. He already had a big erection and he ground it against my belly. "Don't change anything about you, Pinky. You've got exactly the right biological and physical makeup. It's like Frankenstein created you in the lab just for me."

"Just for you?" I croaked. "Exactly right biological and physical makeup?"

He palmed my breast with one hand and squeezed my ass with his other hand. "See? Perfect. Fleshy, yet firm. You're beautiful, Pinky. And more than that, you're the sexiest woman I have ever had the pleasure to be with. Strike that. The sexiest woman that I could've ever conjured in my imagination."

I swallowed with difficulty. "Wow, you do foreplay good."

"You like it? I've been playing around with it for a while and thought I would try it out this morning. Now let's get this party going. How about you turn around and bend over?"

"In the shower? What if I drown?"

elise sax

He smirked his normal little smirk. "Don't worry. I know CPR. If you drown, I'll bring you back to life."

"Yeah, like I believe that. You're not going to give me CPR if you haven't finished yet, if you know what I mean."

Spencer scratched his chin. "You have a point, Pinky. I guess I'll just lift you up against the tile and do you like that."

"Do me?"

Spencer shrugged and smirked his little smirk, again. "Don't shoot me, Pinky. I haven't worked out the rest of my foreplay speech. How's 'making love'? Or 'fucking your guts out'? I like 'fucking'. There's a certain poetry to it."

"Sure. Let's go with that."

With the words out of the way, Spencer's hands were all over me. He caressed his way down the front of my body and slipped a finger inside me. He was getting me ready, but the joke was on him. I had been ready since I had woken up in bed in his arms.

Spencer was ready, too. He looked like he could chop wood with his penis. He picked me up, and I wrapped my legs around him. He backed me up against the tile wall and entered me.

"Oh," I moaned. It felt really good. Normally we did a lot more foreplay, including tongues and everything that nature provided. But today Spencer was all about getting it done before my appointment.

He was thoughtful like that.

Anyway, I didn't need a lot of lips and tongues. By the time that he thrust three times inside me, I felt the familiar rush of pleasure through my body as it rose to orgasm.

Geez, I loved orgasms. They were even better than chocolate.

Thirty minutes later, we were downstairs in the kitchen. Spencer was dressed for work in a tailored Armani suit, his hair perfectly coiffed, and his beard was scruffy and barely visible. I was wearing black pants and a blue top. That was fancy for me.

I put on the coffee, and Spencer sliced the bagels and tossed them into the toaster.

"Orange juice?" he asked. One of the changes that Spencer had implemented was no more bottled orange juice. He insisted on making it fresh every morning.

"Sure," I said. He squeezed the orange juice, and I cracked eggs into a pan.

When the food was ready, we sat down at the table and faced each other. Spencer smirked his little smirk, and I blushed. "Love that," he said. "Love that I can make my wife blush. And I plan on making you blush every second we're on our honeymoon." He checked his watch. "Countdown, Pinky. I can smell the sea air already. Just a few more hours before we leave town and sail the high seas of love." He broke into the Love Boat theme, singing off key.

We had been given a honeymoon cruise as a wedding gift from my best friend Lucy and her husband Harry. Spencer and I had been planning all the things that we were going to do on the cruise, and none of them involved shuffleboard or hanging out on the Lido deck with Captain Stubbing.

Most of our plans entailed new ways to get naked together and pushing the boundaries of lovemaking. I had secretly bought new racy négligées, one outfit for each night, and I had them delivered to my other best friend Bridget's house so that it would remain a surprise for Spencer. I was going to pick them up from her at Tea Time after the match greet.

After Spencer left to go to work, the match greet happened exactly as I had foreseen. Jake got a flat tire, and Molly gave him a ride. They had hit it off at the house, but I knew that they would fall in love in Molly's Honda Fit. It was one of the easiest matches I'd ever done.

With another love match made, I walked to Tea Time, which was my favorite place for coffee. I had a deal with Ruth Fletcher, who owned the tea shop, to give me free lattes for a year. But Ruth was away on an around the world cruise with my grandmother, and she had left Bridget in charge while she was gone.

Tea Time was housed in the center of the historic district. It used to be a saloon, and there were still a few bullet holes in the wall. Bridget was a bookkeeper and she just had a baby, but running the tea shop turned out to be a natural fit.

The social interaction was a relief for her. No longer isolated in her house with the baby, she was now around people all day long. She brought baby Jonathan with her, and he got a lot of attention from the customers.

I walked into the shop. A group of customers were cooing over baby Jonathan, who was perched on the bar in a baby seat. When he was born, Bridget didn't allow anyone to talk to him in baby talk because she thought it would stunt his cerebral cortex. But these days she was giving into it, and I had caught her on more than one occasion calling him her "baby waby."

Bridget waved me over to the bar. I gave Jonathan a kiss on his forehead. "Latte?" Bridget asked, even though I never got anything else to drink. She put her hand over her mouth. "Are you picking up the you-know-whats?" she asked me in her best spy voice.

I nodded.

"Normally, I don't condone women wearing stuff like this to objectify their bodies and make men want them as objects," Bridget said. "But boy, you got some racy, pretty stuff. Sizzle hot!"

I hadn't tried the lingerie on yet, and a little bubble of worry popped inside me. Would I have the nerve to get that down and dirty with Spencer? What if I looked ridiculous in the sexy outfits?

"I put them in bags so you can carry them easier," Bridget explained, putting three large bags on the counter. She made the latte and sat down with me at a table with baby Jonathan on her lap.

"Have you heard from Ruth, lately?" I asked.

"Are you kidding? It's been nonstop. She calls at least twice a day, even though the charges for telephone calls are crazy on that boat. She micromanages everything. When I bought too much

Lapsang Souchong, I thought she was going to have a stroke. I won't make that mistake again. And you know what, Gladie? I think something happened on that cruise. Ruth doesn't seem quite herself. I mean, she's still ornery as hell, but she seems a little different to me."

"I'm Skyping with her and my grandmother in about an hour."

"They discovered Skype?"

"Spencer introduced it to them. But this will be the first time they're placing a call. I'll let you know how it goes." I took a sip of the latte. It was good, but it wasn't quite as good as Ruth's.

"Are you all packed for the cruise, besides the dirty stuff?" Bridget asked.

"Spencer is packed. But I haven't started. I bought three new dresses because they make you dress fancy for dinner." I gnawed on the inside of my cheek. I hadn't done a lot of fancy stuff in my life. I was much more a jeans and t-shirt kind of girl.

Bridget put her hand on mine. "It's going to be wonderful, Gladie. You'll be beautiful, all glammed up, and it's going to be the perfect honeymoon. Even though I don't believe in honeymoons."

I tried to see what the cruise would be like. I was seeing excitement and adventure, but the rest was blurry. I was okay with that. A vacation was a vacation, and I had never been on a real one with Spencer before. I hugged Bridget goodbye and went home. I quickly packed my things, and threw my toiletries into a grocery bag. It took me two minutes to pack completely.

"There. That wasn't so bad," I said, looking appreciatively at my packed suitcase. It was time for the Skype call with my grandmother and Ruth, so I went upstairs to the attic office where my laptop was. As I stepped into my office, I smiled. It was a beautiful sanctuary, filled with antiques and light. Spencer was jealous of my space, and he hinted more than once that he wanted a man cave. I told him that was ridiculous because the whole house was his man cave, but I had secretly planned to have the little room off of the parlor turned into his man cave while we were away on the cruise. It was my wedding gift to him, I mean, besides the hoochie mama underpants.

I turned on my laptop just as the Skype app dinged. I pushed the button and waved at Grandma and Ruth. "Back up a little," I urged. "I'm only seeing cheeks. You have to back up so I can see all of you."

"It's this damn technology. It's the dehumanization of our species. Not that we didn't deserve it," Ruth grumbled as she and Grandma rearranged themselves. It took a good five minutes before they could see me and I could see them.

"You look beautiful, dolly," Grandma said with a smile.

"What are you wearing?" I asked.

"It's called a muumuu. You like it?"

"Of course she doesn't like it, Zelda," Ruth spat. "You look like you're wearing a circus tent. A circus tent made of fifteen colors. Nobody likes it."

"I never realized how comfortable baggy clothes are, dolly.

11

My whole body's breathing. Even my tuchus is breathing. Such a great invention. They wear muumuus here in Fiji."

"Fiji," I breathed. "That sounds like heaven."

"If you call mosquitoes heaven, then yes, it's heaven," Ruth complained. I didn't know what Bridget was talking about. Ruth seemed exactly the same to me.

"Are you all ready for your cruise?" Grandma asked me.

"I just packed. And I matched Molly with Jake."

Grandma clapped her hands together and smiled. "Perfect. What a wonderful love match they are. Good work, Gladie. You've got the gift."

Didn't I know it. I had the gift and how. I could do no wrong.

It was sort of disorienting.

"How's the rest of the cruise?" I asked. "I hear that they have midnight buffets."

"People eating like pigs," Ruth said. "Pigs. They can't get enough. They shovel it in morning, noon, and night. I've never seen anything like it. I don't know how these people don't explode with all the food in their systems. They don't even chew. They just swallow. I saw a man swallow an entire slice of cheesecake, and then he asked for another one. Revolting. I'm not seasick, but I still want to throw up."

"Ruth's a little upset because her friend got off the cruise early," Grandma explained.

"I'm not upset. And you know that I don't have any friends, Zelda."

"What friend?" I asked.

"A man kind of friend," my grandmother said.

"Oh, really? A man friend?"

"Knock that smile off your face, girl," Ruth snapped at me. "You think no man would be interested in me? I'll have you know that I have to fend off advances every day."

"But she didn't fend off this advance," Grandma explained. "Rudolph Varian. A dentist, now retired. He got off early because he's doing a cross-country trip of America, instead."

"That's more of my style," Ruth said, earnestly. "You know, the Grand Canyon, New Mexico, the St. Louis arch. There's a lot to see in our country. We don't have to go to Timbuktu for a little dose of travel and adventure."

Grandma patted Ruth on her back. "There. There. We'll find him, again. We won't let him get too far."

"So, you're going to call the cruise short?" I asked.

"We're talking about it, dolly."

"Spencer and I leave in a couple hours," I said. "I still don't know where we're going. Harry's keeping it a surprise. I can't get a reading on it."

"We're not machines, bubbeleh. We have the third eye, but

the third eye doesn't see everything."

"Third eye, my Aunt Fanny," Ruth said. "She didn't warn me off the clams, and we know how that turned out."

Grandma shrugged her shoulders. "No one bats a thousand, Ruth. Have a nice time on your cruise, dolly. Take lots of pictures."

"And don't make a pig of yourself like the rest of them," Ruth insisted. "Wait until you see the pigs at the troughs. Disgusting. Gross. I don't know why people on cruises are allowed to live. Consume consume consume. All they do is try to get as much food in them as possible. It's nauseating. It's repulsive. It's a crime against nature."

"Don't worry, Ruth," my grandmother said. "We'll find him. We'll chase him down and find him."

Since Spencer was leaving his car behind at the station, I went to pick him up from work. He was only working a half day, just enough time to give last-minute orders to his people. I walked into the station, and Fred, the desk sergeant, greeted me. "Hello, Underwear Girl," he said. "Gee, you sure do look pretty today."

"Thanks, Fred. How's Julie?"

"Oh, she's fine. She's out of the hospital. It turned out that they could save her toe. It's a miracle, really. I was sure that toe was a goner."

He mentioned something about a bagel slicer incident, but I didn't have time to get into details. "Tell her hi for me. And I'm glad about the toe."

Fred buzzed me in back, and I walked down the hall to Spencer's office. I stopped just outside because he was giving orders to his two detectives, Remington and Margie, and I wanted to give them their privacy.

"No problem, boss," I heard Remington say. "I got you, Mr. OG."

"I've got the schedule done," Margie said. "And I moved my needlepoint group meetings until after you get back. So, I'll give my total devotion to the security of the town, chief."

"That's what I want to hear," Spencer said.

Everything was going to plan. I hadn't found a dead person in over a month. The town hadn't been invaded by any cults or crazy people. I was doing a whiz-bang matchmaking job. And Spencer's police force was almost competent. It looked like smooth sailing for our trip.

Peeking in, I got a little thrill watching Spencer give commands. I liked that he was a good police chief and was devoted to his work. I also liked knowing what he looked like naked. Spencer caught my eye, and as if he knew what I was thinking, he gave me his little smirk and waggled his eyebrows like Groucho Marx.

Oh, yes. He looked good naked.

As soon as Spencer was done, I drove us home and parked

my Oldsmobile Cutlass Supreme in the driveway. Lucy and her husband Harry arrived soon after to take us to the cruise terminal in Long Beach.

"We still don't know where we're going," I told Lucy as Harry and Spencer lugged the suitcases to Harry's Bentley.

"Harry won't tell me," Lucy said. "He did say something about not making eye contact with the crew. I don't know what that means." Lucy pulled me aside and whispered, "Tell me the truth. Do I look fat? Do I look fat? How fat do I look? Don't lie to me. I mean, don't lie to me unless you think I need to be lied to. Do I need to be lied to? Am I that fat?"

"No," I said, truthfully. "You don't even look pregnant. I wish my stomach was as flat as yours. You don't have an ounce of cellulite anywhere on your body. Your face is aging in reverse. You're Benjamin Button in a peach organza dress and designer shoes."

Lucy exhaled, as if she had been holding her breath, and kissed me on the cheek. "You're the best friend a woman could ever have."

We piled into the Bentley. Harry started it up, and Frank Sinatra began to sing on his fancy stereo system.

"Now, this isn't your normal kind of cruise," Harry explained, as he drove out of town. "But you don't want any of that froufrou pansy stuff. This is a real man's cruise."

What the hell did that mean? A real man's cruise? I wasn't a real man. I wasn't even a part-time, so-so man. Spencer took my hand and brought it to his lips. I reminded myself to sit back and relax. I was on my honeymoon with the man I love. And what could go wrong on a cruise?

CHAPTER 2

"See a penny. Pick it up. And all day long you'll have good luck." Look around you. Do you have pennies in your life? Little treasures that you overlooked? Be aware of gifts and opportunities. Don't take them for granted. When something good is at your feet, pick it up. Cherish it. Gratefulness is the key to happiness.

Lesson 3, Heart Advice from
Gladie Burger

The cruise ship looked nothing like the Love Boat. It was a lot smaller, and it looked more like a cargo ship than a cruise ship. And I couldn't make out the name of the boat because it was written on the side in Russian.

"Will it float?" I asked at the ship's terminal before we boarded.

"It's seasoned," Uncle Harry explained. "Experienced. That's better than new and shiny."

I had my doubts about that, but I didn't want to act ungrateful in the face of Harry's gift. It turned out that the "cruise ship" was a Soviet-era boat that had been renovated by a Russian billionaire oligarch whose interior design tastes leaned heavily toward gold-plated faucets and velvet wallpaper.

Our stateroom was a good example of that. It had a king-size bed with a black and gold duvet. The walls were covered in purple velvet wallpaper and copies of colorful Impressionist paintings. There was a small bathroom that had mirrors on the walls, and the ceiling and the trim was all about the gold. "Black towels," Spencer said, running his hand over a thick towel in the bathroom.

"Gold toilet paper roll," I said, pointing at the small toilet.

The room was gaudy but luxurious and clean, and I couldn't complain, especially since Spencer was already stripping out of his clothes. "This is going to be good."

I backed up until my legs hit the bed. "We don't even know where we're going. We haven't gotten the list of activities from the cruise director."

"I've already got a list of our activities. You want to see it? I've alphabetized it. There's a lot of L entries, believe it or not."

He stripped down to his boxer briefs, and he smirked his little smirk. "You ready, Pinky? You ready for the alphabet?"

"I was never very good at school."

"I'll tutor you."

"I don't do well at tests."

"Don't worry. No written tests. Only oral. O-R-A-L."

I made a strangled sound, as I tried to swallow. "Okay. I guess we can hold off on the cruise director."

He crossed toward me in two strides and pushed me onto the bed. "This is going to be good," he said, and I believed him.

But before there was a chance to get good, the door to the stateroom opened, and a short, boxer-looking man in his forties came in. He was wearing a purple cruise ship uniform, and he had a crew-cut hairstyle. The muscles on his short limbs bulged through his clothes. His eyes flicked for a second over Spencer's body, which was poised to pounce on me.

"I'm Bruno," he said in a French accent. "I am your steward. I'm here to unpack."

He went to our suitcases and opened them. "Can't it wait?" Spencer asked.

"I unpack and then see if you need anything else. Women? Drugs?"

"Women? Drugs?" Spencer repeated.

"Men, too? You like men?" he asked Spencer with more than a hint of hope in his voice.

Spencer walked into the bathroom and picked up his pants. He put his hand in one of the pockets and came out with his wallet. He handed Bruno a twenty-dollar bill. "Fuck off," Spencer told him with a smile.

Bruno took the money. "Yes, sir." He ducked out of the stateroom, and Spencer double-locked the door behind him.

"Where were we?" he asked me.

"Hold on a second." I took the negligee bag out of my suitcase and went into the bathroom, closing the door behind me. I put on the light blue crotchless bodysuit with the built-in push-up bra. I messed up my hair and swiped a coat of red lipstick on my lips. I looked up at the ceiling mirror and got a good look at my cleavage.

I looked like a whore.

Perfect.

I opened the door and posed for Spencer. His eyes grew big and dark. "Is it my birthday?" he asked. "Did I win a contest? Oh my God, am I dead and gone to heaven?"

"Yes. All three things."

Spencer stripped out of his boxer briefs, ripped the duvet off the bed and leaped onto it. He sat with his back against the headboard. He clapped his hands together.

"Okay, baby, walk sexy to me."

I giggled. "Okay. Like this?" I put my hands on my hips and

took two steps.

"That's working for me. Lean over a little." I giggled, again and shook my boobs at him. Spencer sucked in air and ran his hand over his hair. "That's it. That's it. Oh, thank you, Pinky. Thank you. Now talk dirty to me."

I walked as sexy as I could around the bed toward him and put one foot up on the bed. "Oh, I'm going to talk dirty to you."

He wrapped his hand around my ankle. "Oh, yeah. Oh, yeah. Talk dirty to me, baby. All the dirty."

"That's right. I'm going to talk dirty to you."

"Talk dirty to me."

"I'm going to talk dirty to you."

"Talk dirty to me."

"Oh, yes. I'm going to talk dirty to you."

Spencer squeezed my leg. "Pinky, when do you plan on starting this dirty talk?"

"I'm thinking. I'm thinking. I'm not good at improvisation."

"Anything would do," Spencer said. "Truly. I'm a sure thing."

"Okay, I've figured it out," I said. "I'm ready to talk dirty."

Spencer leaned back and put his hands behind his head with his fingers interlocked. "All righty. Talk dirty to me, sexy baby."

"Here I go," I said in my best Marilyn Monroe voice. "Boner. Boner. Boner, boner, boner. Boooooo....ner." I put my foot down. "How was that? Was it dirty enough for you?"

"Perfect," Spencer growled and pulled me on top of him.

"When is the ship going to leave port?" I asked. Spencer and I were lying on the bed, our limbs tangled, in a dehydrated exhausted heap.

"We've been sailing for hours."

"We have? I haven't felt a thing."

Spencer slapped my butt. "That's because we were rocking the bed the whole time."

"I'm hungry. Can we order room service?"

He leaned over and took a pamphlet off the nightstand. "No room service," he said, reading. "I guess they have a girls and drug service, but they draw the line at food. But dinner's being served in twenty minutes. Just enough time to get cleaned up. You game, or you want to try some more sexy talk?"

"Dinner sounds good."

We dressed up and took the elevator down to the dining room. "I want steak and caviar and chocolate cake," I said, as we rode down. "Do you think they'll have that? Is it a buffet?"

"Beats me. But I bet they have lots of food."

We waited to be seated. There was a large sign with "Welcome Health and Fitness League" written on it. Another sign welcomed the Psychedelics Society to their best "alternative reality."

There wasn't a buffet. It was a formal dinner seating, and we were seated at the Captain's table along with the ship's doctor and six other passengers. The other tables were all filled, and waiters were pouring wine into glasses.

"You're the only passengers who aren't exercising or taking LSD," the captain told the diners at our table. "So, I thought it would be nice to gather you together. I am Captain Boris Mirov, and this is Dr. Jacques Patient."

We went around the table, introducing ourselves. There was an older couple from Russia, a woman from Uzbekistan, two young women from Los Angeles who seemed shocked to find themselves on a Soviet-era boat instead of Princess Cruises, and a short, homely Swiss man, who sat next to me.

The waiter served the first dish. "Pate," Spencer whispered to me.

The chef, who could have been a runway model, approached our table. He winked at one of the L.A. girls, which delighted her but upset her friend. "Tonight I have a wonderful meal prepared for you," he announced and winked at the other L.A. girl, making the first one upset.

The captain introduced the chef. "This is Paolo Macron. He's the best chef we've ever had. But this has been a challenging cruise for him."

"Half the ship doesn't eat starch, fat, or sugar, and the other half of the ship won't eat anything that can be mistaken for a face. But for you, I'm pulling out all the stops. King Louis didn't eat better before his head was cut off."

"I just want a bowl of muesli," the Swiss man next to me said and pushed his plate of pate away from him.

The chef sighed and winked at one of the L.A. girls, but I had lost track of which one he was flirting with. He was so good-looking that he could have successfully flirted with both of them at the same time, if they had been amenable. But they didn't seem amenable.

The food was delicious. After the third course, Bruno the steward tapped Spencer on the shoulder. "So, you're Spencer Bolton? Any relation to Peter Bolton?"

"He's my brother," Spencer said.

"Why didn't you say that before?" Bruno handed Spencer his watch and a pair of my earrings. "Peter's a great guy. Tell him hello for me when you see him."

Bruno walked away, and Spencer and I looked down at the ill-gotten goods that our thief steward had returned. "It's good to know people," I said.

"Peter has a lot of dubious friends," Spencer explained. "He would get along here like a house on fire."

We scanned the dining room. The health and fitness passengers were eating vegetables and green juice. They looked happy, but I gave them two days on their diets before they got mean. The psychedelic group came in all shapes and sizes and walks of life. There were some weirdo hippy people, but most of them seemed normal enough. They were eating a variety of soft food with no faces as a precaution against bad trips.

But the crew looked like it came directly out of the Russian mob. Scarred, tattooed with assorted limps and one-eyes, they looked like they would have known Spencer's super spy brother Peter. Spencer touched my thigh and leaned into me.

"Don't worry, Pinky. If they try to sell you as a sex slave, I'll stop them." His voice started out jokey, but wound up on the serious side. He tugged at his collar and gave nervous looks at our ship's captain and doctor. They didn't seem like Boy Scouts any more than the rest of the crew. "I might have to have a conversation with Harry when all this is over," Spencer continued.

"The food's good, though," I told him. "Mobsters sure know how to eat."

A man at one of the psychedelics table screamed. "Face! Face!" he yelled and hopped onto the table, kicking the dishes to the floor.

"Damned mashed potatoes!" a man yelled and tried to swipe at the man on the table.

"You can take Gladys out of Cannes, but you can't take Cannes out of Gladys," Spencer mumbled.

"Hey, I have nothing to do with that man's psychedelic trip," I said. "And don't call me Gladys. That's a divorceable offense."

The man jumped off the table and ran screaming out of the dining room. The other man approached the captain and wagged his finger at him. "I told you no faces," he growled.

"Mr. Martin, come and drink with us and forget your problems," the captain urged, guzzling his own drink.

There was another scream, and Mr. Martin ran off to save the other passenger.

"Mr. Martin is in charge of the psychedelics," the captain told our table. "He brought an enormous amount of mushrooms on board, in case you'd like some."

"Don't you dare, Pinky," Spencer whispered in my ear.

"They better catch that guy fast," I told him. "He's about to think he sees Aquaman and jump overboard."

"Is that the witch talking?"

"I'm not a witch. And yes, that's the witch talking."

CHAPTER 3

All of us want a relationship that's smooth sailing. Nobody wants problems. But anything worthwhile hits a wave now and then. The secret to a happy ending is riding out the choppy, bad weather, knowing that the smooth sailing will come around again.

Lesson 4, Heart Advice from
Gladie Burger

As first cruises go, mine wasn't half bad. I realized pretty quickly that you don't need a cruise for a honeymoon because all we did was have sex in bed. In other words, any room with a bed and a lock could have served us just as well. The only time we left our stateroom was to go to meals.

We were allowed a table to ourselves for breakfast and lunch, but dinner was all about the Captain's table. Chef Paolo Macron continued to make gourmet meals for us, dietetic meals for the dieters, and more or less nothing for the psychedelics, who had drifted off on their own schedules. Many of the mushroom eaters stayed in their rooms, while others laid out on the deck. Still others wandered around the boat, following invisible people, which was unfortunate for the health and fitness people, who had more than one Jazzercise class interrupted by a high hippy.

But Spencer and I were happily sequestered in our own little world for the most part and only had to deal with the cruise craziness getting to and from our meals.

On our third day, I was inspecting a torn negligee, and Spencer was inspecting my ass. We had lost a significant amount of weight, despite eating three big, gourmet meals every day. Spencer and I were normally sexually active with each other, but we weren't wasting any time on our honeymoon.

"I haven't been this thin since I moved in with my grandmother," I said.

"My shoes are too big now. I've gone up three notches on my belt. Sex is so much better than Crossfit."

Spencer was right. Sex was pretty good. The weight loss was a bonus. In terms of national averages, we now had a six year head-start on our marriage in the sex department.

It turned out that our cruise ship was on its way north and then returning without any day trips or stopping for gas. Our steward Bruno told Spencer that the captain canceled the normal ports of call because of an issue he had with law enforcement. It had to do either with drug smuggling or money laundering. Whatever it was, the captain wasn't taking any chances. A day before we were set to return to Long Beach, the captain was going to leave the ship and escape arrest. But for now, the captain seemed unconcerned that the cops wanted him in jail.

"Pretty much the entire crew is wanted somewhere around the world, Pinky," Spencer explained to me. "These guys aren't boy scouts."

Despite the Jazzercise enthusiasts, the mushroom-eating bad trippers, and the gangster crew, it was a great cruise. "Honeymoons are a great start to a marriage," I told Spencer in bed, as we laid there, exhausted and thinner. "Everyone should do it. It's like starting off a meal with chocolate cake."

"I've got your chocolate cake right here, baby," he flirted, but he was too exhausted to really mean it. Even Michael Phelps takes a break from swimming, occasionally.

"We should get a thank you gift for Harry. It was so sweet of him to give us this cruise as a wedding present."

"We'll take him out for dinner when we get back. He won't want a souvenir t-shirt," Spencer said.

I kissed Spencer's shoulder and then froze. A grim sensation crawled up my body and took over my respiratory system, making it hard to breathe. "Bomb," I said when I could finally draw breath, again.

Spencer sat up in bed. "Bomb?"

"Bomb cyclone."

"What's a bomb cyclone?"

All of a sudden, the ship pitched violently. Our belongings went flying, as if there was a tornado in our stateroom. We were Dorothy, but we were on the high seas. Visions of Titanic and The Poseidon Adventure filled my mind. The ship rocked and rolled with a vengeance.

"I don't want to die like this," I moaned.

"You're not going to die. It's just a little turbulence."

"Turbulence is for planes. This is something else. This is The Perfect Storm. This is The Creature from the Black Lagoon but you know, with big waves that are going to sink us. Sink us, Spencer! You know that I can't hold my breath very long."

"You'll be fine."

"Bull hockey. I'm pretty sure if this ship goes over, it's a good fifteen-minute swim to get out from under it. You know perfectly well that I can't hold my breath for more than thirty seconds. Thirty seconds is a lot less than fifteen minutes!"

"Calm down. We're going to be fine," he insisted, his face growing greener as I looked at him. "I'm going to...I'm going to..."

And then he ran for the bathroom. But with the violent rocking of the boat, Spencer couldn't get there in time. "Pinky!" he yelled, as if he was apologizing, and then he threw up our gourmet breakfast all over my open suitcase.

Whatever nightmare had our cruise ship in its clutches, it seemed to increase in strength and intensity. "We better get out of here, Pinky." Spencer had to crawl to get to his clothes. He tossed me a pair of his sweatpants and a t-shirt to put on. We were rocking and rolling, violently. I crawled to Spencer and handed him an ice bucket.

"Just in case," I told him.

He opened the door, and we crawled out into the hallway. There, it was bedlam. Passengers were struggling to walk and not having much luck. Man was falling on woman. Woman was falling on man. A couple people I recognized as Jazzercisers were screaming that the ship was going down and we were all going to die. Spencer and I didn't try to walk. We continued to crawl down the hallway toward the elevator, avoiding the falling passengers.

It wasn't easy. The cruise had turned into a carnival ride with no end. The screaming got louder, and by the time that we made it to the elevator, Spencer had thrown up again, this time in the ice bucket he was carrying. Afterward, he left it in the corner of the hallway. Luckily, the elevator doors opened, and we crawled inside. I managed to stand long enough to push the button. Two other passengers made it inside and fell down. The doors closed, and the room was filled with Frank Sinatra singing, "My Way."

"We're going to die," one of the other passengers cried.

"No, we're not," Spencer moaned. He didn't sound convinced, and his face was a dark shade of green.

"Shut up, liar," the woman moaned at him. "We're going to die. And I heard that they don't have life vests on this rusty tub. And

I heard they only have enough lifeboats for the crew. And I heard that this is shark-infested waters."

"I wouldn't worry about the sharks," I said. "You'll get hypothermia and die before the sharks get you."

Spencer caught my eye, a wave of terror washing over his face. "Guessing," I told him. I wasn't having a third eye moment. I wasn't seeing anything, but the woman was annoying me with her doomsday talk. I didn't need any more anxiety than I already had. If anyone was going to freak out, it was going to be me.

The elevator dinged, the doors opened, and Frank Sinatra stopped singing. Spencer and I crawled out into the reception area, but the other two passengers tried to stand without luck. We didn't look back, though. It was all we could do not to get killed as we crawled our way through the room toward the windows. The rocking wasn't letting up. Belongings, dishes and glasses, and just about everything else was flying through the air, taking out people left and right.

And there was vomiting.

Lots of vomiting.

The crew didn't seem to be the least bit concerned, however. They managed to walk just fine, and they moved around, trying to help the distressed passengers.

"Hello, Mr. and Mrs. Bolton," the captain said, looking down at us as we crawled on the floor. He seemed totally unbothered by the rocking of the ship, and he stood upright without any balance problems.

"What's happening?" Spencer asked him. "Is the ship going down?"

"No, no," the captain said, happily. "Just a little bomb cyclone. Nothing to worry about. This ship has seen a million of them. It'll pass."

At the words "bomb cyclone," Spencer locked eyes with me and mouthed witch at me. I ignored him. "How long until it passes?" I asked the captain. "An hour? Two?"

"Oh, God, please don't let it be two hours," Spencer moaned. He was completely green, and he kept clutching his stomach, as if he could stop it from roiling.

"Hard to say," the captain said. "One. Maybe two days."

"Days?" Spencer asked. "Days?" His voice rose an octave, and he got even greener.

"Exciting, isn't it?" the captain asked.

Dr. Patient plopped down on a chair next to us. "What a nightmare. I need a drink. The passengers are not happy. The ship is rocking to the left and then to the right and then to the left and then to the right. This motion of the ship makes some people sick." Spencer moaned and put his hand over his mouth. "Do you know what I'm saying?" the doctor continued. "Rocking to the left, rocking to the right, rocking to the left. Up, down, up, down. You see how that could make a person with a gentle stomach a little sick?" Spencer put his head between his knees, and I thought I heard him crying, but I wasn't sure.

"Doctor, can you help my husband? He's very sick," I told him.

"What's the matter?" the doctor asked Spencer. "Is the rolling, rolling, rolling of the ship causing you distress? Is the bile moving up your throat with the wild pitching of the boat? Do you feel overwhelmed, as if your body is betraying you, ready to make you spasm in agony as all of your fluids spew out of you?"

"Yes, on all of those counts. Pinky, make him stop," Spencer moaned.

The doctor opened his doctor bag, popped a pill under Spencer's tongue and gave him a shot in his butt. "You're not allergic to shellfish, are you?" he asked after he gave him the shot.

He didn't wait for an answer. Things had degenerated around us. The entire deck level had been invaded by terrified and sick passengers, prepared to abandon ship. When they found out we weren't going to die—at least not from sinking into the ocean—they focused on their nausea, dizziness, and general discomfort. We were being rocked like a dog shaking a chew toy, and I couldn't imagine two more days like this. Passengers were projectile vomiting and crying. It was like a World War One movie.

The weirdest thing was that I felt perfectly fine. I couldn't walk upright, but I wasn't the least bit nauseated. Spencer was still green, but he was better since the doctor treated him. With so many people in distress, and the captain unconcerned about their plight,

Spencer went into high gear. Perhaps it was his role as police chief or maybe it was just the way he was, but he took command and began to organize help for the passengers.

He staggered away with the doctor to get started, and I sat cross-legged on the floor next to the captain. Two health and fitness people approached, falling onto two chairs next to him. They turned out to be Muffy and Buffy, the head of the Health and Fitness League. They asked him if we were going down like the Titanic, and he explained about the bomb cyclone.

"It's great for weight loss," Muffy said, happy. "They're tossing their cookies, and they're not eating a thing."

"Thank goodness," Buffy added. "That chef of yours has been sneaking in naughty foods. He says they're dietetic, but they're not. You should fire him. He's pushing fat and sugar onto my guests!"

"Time to steer the ship," the captain muttered and walked away, easily navigating the rocking floor beneath his feet.

"Come on, Muffy," Buffy said. "We'll give them the lecture against bulimia. We don't want them throwing up after this."

"But this is golden," Muffy said. "I bet we get an average ten-pound loss. Think of the Yelp ratings!"

"I'm not feeling so well," Buffy complained.

"Me, either. I shouldn't have eaten that salad dressing. I wonder when the ship is going to stop rocking."

They stumbled away. Spencer had disappeared, and I was alone. There was still pandemonium and a lot of panicked passengers, but under Spencer's command, the crew had finally started to really help them, allaying their fears and handing out buckets for the vomiting.

Lots of vomiting.

A door opened, and wind blew through the room with a loud howling noise. I hadn't seen what was going on outside yet, and I wanted to know just how bad it was. The captain had assured everyone that we were safe, but he wasn't exactly a trustworthy guy. I crawled to the wall and pulled myself up, holding tight to the windowsill for balance.

Outside was a rolling wall of water. The ship was being tossed in the waves like it was a toy boat and not a large cruise ship. "Like Disneyland," Bruno said, coming up next to me. "I was there two years ago. Fun, but the food was too expensive. Although, the pockets made up for it."

"Pockets?"

"Americans with their wallets in the back pocket. Such sweet, trusting people."

I blinked and thought back to our belongings abandoned in our open stateroom. Bruno was a thief, but he liked Spencer's brother, so hopefully we would return home with our wallets.

If we returned home.

"Is this dangerous?" I asked Bruno, pointing at the waves outside.

"This is nothing. This ship cuts ice in the Arctic. It fought Hitler. Hitler was much worse than water. Water is nothing compared to Hitler."

"Hitler was bad," I agreed, watching the water hit the windows. "But I don't think people will be able to handle this for much longer."

"The captain's going to turn the ship back to Long Beach, but he has to move out of the bomb cyclone first."

Bruno was called away to help a woman. The ship pitched forward, and I fell to my knees. I looked around for Spencer, but I couldn't find him. There were fewer people in the room, and I crawled to an open spot on a comfortable looking couch. As I got closer, I recognized the chef, Paolo Macron, sitting there, staring straight ahead.

Pulling myself up to sit down, I saw what he was staring at. From the couch, we had an amazing view of the horror outside. "Crazy, right?" I said to him. He nodded slightly. "I hope this ends fast. People are so sick. It's like the time when I worked at the sausage and pepper stand at an outdoor market in Butte, Montana. That was bad. Who knew that salmonella could live at those temperatures? I almost took the entire town out." I bit my lip. "You won't pass that along, will you? My husband doesn't need to know that little anecdote about me."

Macron was noncommittal. I guessed it was a juicy bit of

gossip to know that I almost killed a city of fried meat enthusiasts. Oh, well. Spencer knew worse than that about me.

People walked by us, slamming against the windows as they lost their balance. The two L.A. girls passed, holding onto each other for support. "Holy cow, they're giving you the evil eye," I told the chef. "What did you do? Did you get involved with one of them? Not smart, chef. Not smart at all. They look like they want to kill you. You better hide your knives."

He didn't answer and kept staring ahead. "I'm sorry. That was out of line," I said. "I didn't mean to pry into your personal life."

He nodded and then his head lobbed to the side. "Chef Macron? Are you okay? Are you feeling sick?" I asked.

His head fell forward, and then as if in slow motion, the rest of his body followed, and he fell onto the floor. "Chef? Chef, are you okay?"

I looked around for the doctor, but he wasn't there. I scooted down onto the floor. "Chef? Chef? Are you sick?" I asked.

That's when I saw the shrimp fork jabbed deep in his carotid artery.

The chef had been shrimped to death.

CHAPTER 4

Love is about patience. The more patient you are, the easier it is to love for the long term. He leaves the cap off the toothpaste. She shops every sale. Patience. You might start off thinking your spouse hung the moon, but that wears thin when he leaves his dirty underpants on the floor. In these times, take a deep breath and muster all of your patience reserves. Then, remember the love, remember the man beyond his dirty underpants. That's how love goes on.

Lesson 5, Heart Advice from
Gladie Burger

"Are you kidding me?"

"It's not my fault."

"I thought you were done with this stuff."

"It's not my fault."

"What's that in his neck? One of those little things to hold corn on the cob?"

"I think it's a shrimp fork."

"No, I think it's definitely the corn on the cob thing."

"Listen, Spencer. One thing I know about is food. It's a shrimp fork."

"People eat shrimp with forks?" he asked. "How is that logical?"

"I think we're veering off the subject, here. I don't think the shrimp fork is important in the scheme of things."

"It's important, Pinky. Now we know that he was killed by a moron who uses a tiny fork to eat shrimp instead of with his hands like a normal person."

"So, you're saying that the killer may not be totally normal?" I asked him. "Is that your sharp law enforcement instinct talking?"

The ship pitched sharply, and I fell forward, tripping over poor Chef Macron's body and knocked into Spencer like a linebacker, sending us both flying onto the couch. Spencer struggled to right himself and pulled me onto his lap. He put his forehead against mine.

"Are you being haughty, Pinky?"

"I don't know. I don't know what that means."

"It means giving me shit. Are you giving me shit?"

"Yes."

"Tell me about the man with the fork in his neck."

"I had a whole conversation with him," I said.

"When he was dead?"

I pushed off his lap. "Don't judge me."

Spencer arched an eyebrow. "You had a whole conversation with a dead man?"

"The ship is moving a lot. It made him nod and move. He didn't seem dead." Spencer nodded. "And then he fell over in this position, and I saw the shrimp fork."

Spencer had ordered the crew to cordon off the reception area. The ship was still rocking like it was going to break in half, but the panic had died down. The passengers were sent to their staterooms, and the doctor was making house calls, shooting everyone up with anti-nausea medicine. That is, all except for the psychedelic folks who didn't seem to be seasick at all. They even walked surefooted like the boat wasn't rocking. Spencer was better than he had been, but he was still a light shade of green, and he was dehydrated.

I felt guilty about the dead chef because since I had gotten the gift from my grandmother, I hadn't found one dead body, and I thought my sleuthing days were behind me. But here I was finding another murdered guy. And the worst thing was that the sleuth bug was biting again, and I wanted more than anything to find out who killed Paolo Macron and why.

And I was on my honeymoon.

It took nearly an hour for the doctor to show up. The captain came, too, and where he was lackadaisical about the bomb cyclone, he wanted the whole murder thing to go away in a hurry. In fact, he was adamant that it wasn't murder.

"No, no, no," the captain insisted. "This is suicide. I've seen it before. The waves made him seasick, so he killed himself."

"He jabbed a shrimp fork into his own neck?" Spencer asked, sarcastically.

"Western Europeans are very emotional," the captain explained.

"I think he was murdered," I said.

"Shhh," the captain urged. "Let's just keep this among ourselves. Murder isn't good for the cruise business. The bosses wouldn't like it." He put his hand up to his throat in a defensive gesture. I could only imagine who the bosses were.

"It looks like murder," the doctor said, examining the body. "Strange murder. Normally we see murder by a forty-five or at least a machete. Isn't that right, Captain?"

"Nobody I know would kill a man with a shrimp fork," the captain agreed. "It must be a health and fitness passenger. There aren't a lot of calories in shrimp. My wife eats shrimp when she's on a diet. She's always on a diet. But she's big as a house. A large house. Maybe she shouldn't eat shrimp. I don't know. I never diet. Russian men don't diet, you know. I like shrimp, though."

We stared at poor Chef Paolo Macron's dead body with the shrimp fork in his neck, like we were wondering if he had enjoyed the appetizer. He was very handsome, and he was a nice guy, but I bet there were all kinds of people who wanted him dead. The two L.A. girls, for example, didn't seem too happy with his player ways. Not to mention Muffy and Buffy, who were irked by his rich food. Those were just the ones that I knew about. I was sure that a little investigation would uncover a whole slew of suspects. It wouldn't be hard. I had a captive audience. I could make quick work of them, asking questions and getting to the bottom of this.

My mind raced with the questions I would ask. First of all, I needed more information about the chef. Who was he and why would someone want him dead besides the fact that he was a Don Juan and a fattening food-pusher?

"No, Pinky. No."

I blinked out of my sleuthing reverie. "What?"

"I know that look, Pinky," Spencer said. "It's the butting your nose in and risking your life look. You're not going to investigate the murder of the chef of a Russian ship in the middle of a bomb cyclone. Do you hear me?"

I stood up with my feet planted wide apart on the floor so that I wouldn't fall. "Take that back," I ordered him. "I don't butt in. I'm not going to investigate anything. And don't order me around.

elise sax

This isn't your jurisdiction. It's the captain's jurisdiction. Only he can stop me from investigating."

"I don't want you to investigate," the captain said.

"Why?" I whined. "I can help. Don't you want help?"

Spencer slapped his forehead and moaned. It started off as a "why, Gladie, why?" moan but ended as a seasick moan.

"Can you give me another shot?" he asked the doctor.

"My stock is gone. No more anti-nausea medicine," the doctor said.

Spencer gasped and a look of panic passed over his face. "Tell me you're lying to me."

The doctor shrugged, and Spencer looked like he was deciding whether to kill himself or punch the doctor in the nose.

"You should lie down," I told Spencer.

"Yes, my men will handle this," the captain said, gesturing toward the dead body.

Spencer didn't look convinced. "How?"

"First we'll toss him overboard. Get rid of this mess."

"You can't do that," Spencer insisted. "He's a victim of a crime, and I'm sure he has family. Put him in the freezer until we get home."

"I hope the sous chef doesn't think he's the supper special," the captain said, but agreed to preserve the body in the freezer.

I helped Spencer back to our room and put cold compresses on the back of his neck and his forehead to try and stem the nausea. It was no use. He was up all night, as the ship was tossed in the waves. Finally, he fell asleep from exhaustion a little after dawn.

I was still totally fine, and I felt guilty that I was starving and wanted to eat a huge breakfast while Spencer was lying spent and sick in our honeymoon bed. I checked on him one last time in bed. He was snoring lightly, finally getting some relief from his seasickness. It was my moment to get out and grab some food before he woke up again.

Sneaking out of our room, I clicked the door closed softly behind me. Either the boat was rocking slightly less or I had become more adept at maintaining my balance, because I managed to walk to the elevator without crawling or falling.

When I got to the dining room, there was only one large table set for breakfast with only five people sitting down at it. I sat next to Hans Weber, who was eating his bowl of muesli. I ordered eggs benedict and home fried potatoes, hoping that the kitchen could handle my order without their chef.

I also hoped none of my food was stored in the freezer with poor dead Chef Macron.

"I'm so glad to see that you're not seasick," I told Hans.

"It's because I eat old-fashioned muesli instead of the heavy food that's not good for anybody."

"Heavy food is bad," I lied. Was there anything better than heavy food? If there was, I hadn't come across it. What was light food, anyway? Muesli? Fruit? Blech.

"The psychedelic people are eating mushrooms on the deck," the captain told him. "Mushrooms are light. You could join them."

"Mushrooms are light in calories with no fat or gluten," Muffy announced, eating her egg white and spinach omelet. "But those crazy people have already fried off half of their brains with mushrooms. One of them thought one of my fitness guests was Mao Zedong. He was railing like a madman, shouting 'Fuck your communism!' You can imagine how my guest felt. Especially since she was a woman."

It turned out that the health and fitness people were suffering like dogs in their staterooms, but they had all lost much more weight than they had expected, so Muffy was ecstatic. Buffy, however, was in her room with her head in a bucket.

After breakfast, I slipped into the kitchen to try and get some information about the dead chef. Like the rest of the crew, the kitchen staff looked like they had walked out of a mobster movie rather than a cooking school.

"So, did you know Chef Macron? Where was he from? Who was he sleeping with?" I asked everyone the same set of questions, but all I got in return were death stares. It was looking more and more like one of the chef's staff could have stabbed him with a shrimp fork. But why?

"Mrs. Spencer, do you need help?" Bruno asked me, walking into the kitchen. "Maybe a snack? I'll bring it to your room."

"No, thank you, Bruno. I was just helping Spencer with his investigation." Boy, I had lost count of the lies I had told in my life. I was so going to hell, but I couldn't stop myself. My nosy parker self was out in full force.

"What investigation? The drug smuggling or the money laundering?" Bruno asked.

"The murder," I said. Bruno stared at me without blinking. "You know, the chef? The dead guy in the freezer with the shrimp fork in his neck?"

Bruno pointed at me. "Oh, yeah. Paolo." He looked around the kitchen. "Hey, who killed the chef?" he called out. The staff stopped chopping, mixing, and washing. "Luca Three Thumbs, you didn't kill him with a shrimp fork, did you?"

A man with three thumbs approached us, followed by five more of the kitchen staff. He held up a large knife. "Why would I use a shrimp fork? I could use this."

"Me, I use boning knife," a short man with a bandana wrapped around his head announced. "Sharp one. Kills a man good."

"Did you kill him?" I asked.

"Who? Chef? No, I didn't know him yet."

"The chef arrived only a few months ago," Luca Three

Thumbs explained. "Put his dick in everything he could find."

"You mean like fish and cans of pate?" Bruno asked.

"No, I mean ladies," Luca said. The other men nodded in agreement. "Every woman, young or old, fat or thin, tall or short, smart or dumb, he would put his linguine with clam sauce right in. So, he didn't have time to yell at us. Very different from other chefs."

"Oh," I said, disappointed. In other words, every woman on the ship was a suspect. "Where did he come from? Was he running from something or someone?"

Luca shrugged, but the man with the bandana took a step forward. "He was chef in Mexico City. I heard he ran out of there in a hurry. Cartel was after him for banging the wife of one of the big bosses."

The hair on the back of my neck stood on end. The cartel. They had done some meth business in Cannes, and I knew they were not to be crossed. It would stand to reason that they would kill the chef for revenge. But with a shrimp fork?

The staff went back to work. I asked Bruno to bring ginger ale and some hot broth to our room, even though I doubted Spencer could hold it down when he woke up. When I left the kitchen, I bumped into the doctor.

"Did you find more anti-nausea medicine?" I asked him.

"No, but I discovered a treasure trove of morphine. I'm going to knock the ship out right now. There's too much vomiting for the cleaning crew to handle. So, something has to be done."

"I'll come with you," I told him. If I was helping him dole out morphine, I figured I could get into the rooms and ask a lot of questions. "Can we see Spencer first?"

Spencer was still asleep when we got to the room. Bruno was right behind us with the broth and ginger ale. I got some fluids into Spencer, and then the doctor shot him up with happy juice.

"Come ride the rollercoaster of happiness, Pinky," Spencer said and passed out. Bruno helped me to prop him up on two pillows, and I tucked him in.

"All right," I told the doctor. "Let's get to work."

CHAPTER 5

Ask questions. If you love him now, just think how much you'll love him once you get to know everything about him.

Lesson 6, Heart Advice from
Gladie Burger

We went around the ship, knocking people out with drugs. I mean, the doctor knocked them out while I grilled each deathly ill person about whether they knew Chef Macron, and if they had seen anything suspicious.

"Uhhhh. Ohhh. Uhhh," Buffy moaned. She was lying in her bed on her stomach with her head hanging off the side. Dr. Patient got the morphine ready.

"You didn't like that the chef wouldn't prepare low calorie meals," I prompted.

"Being murdered was too good for that bastard. I wish someone would murder me. It would put me out of my misery."

"Were you intimate with him?"

"Are you kidding? I don't want herpes. He went through women like Toyotas go through McDonalds. Billions and billions served. I think he had sex with half of our guests by the second night. Have penis, will travel. He was so…so…I'm going to throw up!"

She threw up, and Dr. Patient shot her full of morphine.

We walked out of the room, and the doctor stopped. "Why do you care so much about this chef man?" he asked me. "Were you involved with him, too?"

"I'm on my honeymoon."

"But were you involved with him?"

"No."

"He was a silly man. He used women; he didn't make love to them." The doctor stepped forward. "I make love to women. I am not a silly man."

"You're not?"

"No. I do not go from one woman to another. When I'm with a woman, I give her all my attention. I please her." He had food between his teeth and a good amount of blackheads on his nose. His breath smelled more than a little like a dirty martini. His pupils were dilated, and he was focused intently on my lips.

"My husband is a police chief. He has a gun," I said.

He opened his doctor bag and took out a large gun. "So do I."

I scratched Dr. Patient off my suspect list. He could have killed the chef with drugs or his gun, so I didn't think he would have resorted to killing him with a shrimp fork. Although, maybe they had a I'm-not-silly-you-are fight, and the shrimp fork was handy.

"I like my husband's gun better," I said, pushing the doctor away from me. The ship was still rocking and rolling, but I was getting better and better at keeping my balance. Luckily, with his attempt at seduction thwarted, the doctor didn't press his luck, and he put his gun back in his bag.

We continued making rounds, and I wasn't getting any closer to finding out who killed the chef. To his credit, the doctor didn't stop for a break, making sure that all of the suffering passengers could get some relief as quickly as possible. By the time we reached the two L.A. girls, I wasn't holding out much hope.

They were both sitting up in bed watching reality TV. They were sick but not too sick, so the doctor didn't shoot them up with morphine. "Hello, there," I said. "Oh, this is a good episode." I had never seen it, but I was trying to bond with them over screaming women with hair extensions.

"I hate her," one of the girls said. "She's such a poser."

"Yeah, a poser," I agreed.

"She thinks she's all that, but she's so not," the other girl said.

"So not," I agreed. "Kind of like the chef. What a poser. So not all that."

Their focus shifted from the television for the first time, and they locked eyes with me. "We're over that guy," one of them said.

"So over. Way over," the other said.

They exchanged glances with each other and something passed between them. I recognized it. Friendship. Girl code. They had obviously had a falling out over a man, but they had reached a truce. But I couldn't let them stay quiet.

"He was a big jerk. You must have been angry at him."

"He was a man," one of them sneered and shot a pointed look at the doctor. "We're used to it."

"But he played you. He pitted each of you against the other. He deserved to die!" I accused them of murder, but they didn't seem upset. They broke out their manicure sets and started to remove their nail polish. I changed gears. "Do you know who would want him dead?"

"Anybody who slept with him?" one of them said like a question.

"Was he married? What do you know about his background?"

"Well, he said he was the greatest chef of all time, whatever that means," the other girl said. "I mean, microwave a Hot Pocket much? Like it's so hard to cook."

"Yeah, just GrubHub it and stop your bitching." They both laughed.

"Did he mention a Mexican cartel?" the doctor asked. "I heard he worked in Mexico and had a hard time."

"What's a Mexican cartel?" one of the girls asked. "Is that one of those stick doughnuts?"

"No, that's a churro," I said. I didn't know much about international intrigue, but I knew about desserts.

"I don't know about anything Mexican. He said he was all that, and I don't want to talk about the rest."

"Me either."

When the doctor and I left the room, he turned to me. "They did it," he told me. "Women kill with shrimp forks."

"They do?"

"Yes."

"I've never heard of anyone being murdered with a shrimp fork before. Is it a thing?"

"You know women," he said, as if he was proud of his deductive powers. "They have small hands. A shrimp fork is tiny. Do you see?"

"I don't think you need to have small hands to use a shrimp fork."

"But a man has big hands. He would use a gun or beat a man to death. You see?"

He wasn't wrong. "You're totally wrong. A woman can beat a man to death. I could beat a man to death." The doctor blinked and took a step back.

We finally finished with the passengers. The psychedelics moved on from whatever they were doing on the deck and were now eating egg salad sandwiches in the dining room. It dawned on me that any of the druggies could have killed the chef during some kind of bad trip, but they seemed pretty tame.

It was time to get back to Spencer to see how he was, so I didn't bother talking to the psychedelics, but as I said goodbye to the doctor, Martin, the head of the psychedelics approached me.

"I heard that you're investigating the chef's death."

"Not really investigating," I said.

"Well, it's not any of my guests, so I want you to stay away from them."

I almost stomped my foot. I hated to be told what to do. It was all I could do to stop myself from marching over to his people and accuse them of murder. But it had been hours since Spencer had been knocked out with a narcotic, and I wanted to see how he was doing. More than that, I felt guilty for leaving my sick husband in order to snoop around. Where were my priorities? Miss Marple wouldn't have left her husband to snoop around. What was I talking about? Miss Marple wasn't married, and if she had been married, she would have dropped her hubby the minute a dead body popped up in the library.

"How did you know the chef?" I demanded in my best tough cop voice with my finger in his face. There was no reason to suspect that Martin knew the chef. Besides the fact that they both chopped mushrooms, they didn't have anything else in common. But I was wrong.

"I didn't know him that well," Martin said, surprising me. "We met in Mexico. He was involved in shady dealings, so I stayed away from him."

"You stayed away from him?"

"Okay, fine. I might have done some business with him, but he was trouble. He had dangerous friends, if you know what I mean. I didn't want any part of it. And anyway, I got turned onto the Peyote tourism trade. The rest was history."

I had so many questions. The first questions was: There's a Peyote tourism trade? The other questions had to do with Mexican cartels and which one preferred murder by shrimp fork. But I didn't have time to ask more questions. We were interrupted by the captain, who insisted that I follow him to the kitchen.

As we walked through the dining room, I counted up the suspects. The most obvious ones were every woman on the ship, especially the two L.A. girls. The chef was a skeevy player who parked his penis in every harbor, so to speak. There was no shortage of used and tossed aside women who would have loved to ram a shrimp fork into his neck.

Then, there was Muffy and Buffy, who were upset at the lackluster menu for their dieters. They could have gotten into it with the chef about low carb and low-fat food. He probably came back at them about the importance of butter and cream in everyone's life, and then it went from dicey to deadly. It wouldn't have taken much for one of the fit women to grab a shrimp fork off a table and jab it into the chef's neck.

Passengers aside, the crew of the cruise ship was entirely made up of underworld figures. Any of them could have killed the chef just for the hell of it, or they could have been paid by the cartel to do him in. And what if Martin was lying? Maybe it wasn't a coincidence that he had wound up on the chef's ship. Maybe he was really part of the cartel, sent here to kill the chef.

Murder was horrible. But mysteries made me giddy with excitement. Obviously, I was a terrible person, but I could live with that.

I followed the captain into the kitchen and into the large, walk-in pantry. "How's Spencer?" he asked me.

"I was just going to check on him. The doctor gave him a shot and knocked him out."

"You need to wake him up. We need his investigative skills. We might have a bigger problem. Look around. What do you see?"

I looked around. "I see crates of food. And three rats." I stepped closer to him. "And some cockroaches. Holy cow. A lot of cockroaches. Oh! And another rat. How about we get out of here?"

The captain ignored the vermin. "Look closer. What kind of food?"

"I don't know. There must be a thousand crates or more. And some of the crates are moving." I shuddered. For the first time, I was getting nauseated.

"Okay. I'll tell you what's not here. Shrimp. There's no shrimp. Remember to tell that to your husband. It's a big clue. No shrimp. Now, come with me."

I was happy to leave the rat and cockroach-filled pantry. We went to another room, and this one was filled with linens, china, and cutlery. "Look around," the captain told me. "What do you see?"

"No rats."

"And you know what else isn't here?"

"Jimmy Hoffa."

The captain squinted at me. "Jimmy Hoffa? No. Shrimp forks."

"Shrimp forks?"

"There are no shrimp forks," he said, grabbing a handful of cutlery and letting them drop onto the floor. He was right. There were no shrimp forks.

"What does it mean?" I asked.

"It means that you're right. Chef Macron was murdered. But..."

"It was premeditated," I finished for him. "Somebody brought a shrimp fork onboard, specifically to kill the chef."

It was diabolical. It was also creepy as hell. My skin prickled, and a chill went up my spine. I hugged myself for warmth. The captain gestured at me with his big, sausage fingers.

"Exactly. You have learned much from your husband? Did he teach you the art of deductive reasoning? Are you Dr. Watson to his Sherlock Holmes?"

"Ha! He wishes I were Dr. Watson. Do you have any idea who would have had it in for the chef enough to plan out his murder?"

"Tell Spencer that I barely said ten words to the chef. He was new, you know. Six months. I want to shoot myself for firing the last chef. But the owner wanted a new menu, prettier food like on television."

"And the old chef wouldn't make prettier, TV food?"

"No. He said he didn't do fads. He had worked on this ship for twenty years. He made good borscht for the crew, and wonderful sauces. Good, heavy meals." The captain shrugged. "But the world is a cruel place. The old must make room for the new. What can we do? But the old chef was short and ugly, and he left the passengers alone. None of the Casanova antics of Macron. None of the ego, except in the kitchen, which was fine. I should have fought the owner about the firing. I miss the borscht. No one would have killed that little Swiss chef. No one would have bothered. Oh, well. Please wake up your husband and get him on the case. We have a murderer among us, Mrs. Bolton. A murderer."

With his dramatic pronouncement made, the captain marched out of the kitchen. I urged my gift to get into gear and give me a clue about the murderer. There was something tickling the edges of my brain, but I couldn't see it clearly. I knew that the detail about the shrimp fork was important, but nothing else was jumping out at me. I had no idea who had killed the chef and why.

But now, I knew that the murder weapon wasn't just a handy tool to use in a heated moment. Someone had purposely brought it onboard for the purpose of murder. Why a shrimp fork?

Who owns a shrimp fork, anyway?

Stuck in a dead end, I left to finally go back to my stateroom. Poor Spencer was alone in his sick, drugged state on his honeymoon. But as I walked through the dining room, something inside me made me stop in my tracks.

The ship was still being rocked ruthlessly in the bomb

cyclone, and there were very few diners. The psychedelics were finishing up their meal, and besides them, there were only a handful of other diners. Hans Weber was eating a bowl of muesli, again. I watched him chew. There was no way he was armed with shrimp forks. As far as I could tell, he wouldn't know a shrimp fork from a pizza cutter. He had pushed aside the gourmet food since we arrived on board.

For some reason, I sat next to him. "How are you holding up, Mr…"

"Weber," he finished. "What do you want?"

"Just checking up on you, making sure you're doing well, despite the bomb cyclone."

"I'm fine. Ready for this cruise to be over. I heard we're on our way back, and we arrive tomorrow."

"Is that home for you? Long Beach?"

He narrowed his eyes, and he dropped his spoon into his bowl of muesli. "What do you really want from me?"

"Nothing. I…"

"It's about the murder, isn't it? You've been asking a lot of questions. What do they call it? Busybody. Yes, that's it. You're a busybody. Well, don't busybody me, Missus. I don't know anything about murder. I just want to be left alone."

"A cruise is an odd place to go to be left alone."

He scooted his chair away from me and stood. "I know what this is about. You're targeting me because I'm a foreigner."

"No. I…"

"Foreigners get shabby treatment. We are blamed for all wrongs. We're like Jonah, thrown into the belly of the whale. Well, don't worry. I'm going home as soon as we return to land. You won't have to worry about this foreigner anymore. You won't have me to blame with your busybody ways."

"No… I… No…"

Thankfully, Bruno interrupted us. "Mrs. Bolton, Spencer is asking for you."

I stood up, glad to end the conversation with Hans. "Is he okay?"

Bruno put his hand out and tilted it side to side. "Sort of. I've seen worse."

I left with Bruno. While I struggled to walk through the boat as it rocked and rolled under my feet, I wracked my brain to recall where Hans Weber was from. Since a good chunk of the people on the ship were from another country, his foreigner status didn't strike me as something to remember.

Then, I remembered.

"Muesli," I said out loud. "Who eats muesli, Bruno?"

"Germans. And the Swiss, like that man who was yelling at

you."

Switzerland. That was it. Weber was from Switzerland.

Just like the ship's chef before Macron was hired.

CHAPTER 6

Just because you're paranoid doesn't mean they're not out to get you. In other words, trust yourself. Don't worry if you've had bad judgment in the past. If you know he or she is your soulmate, go with that feeling. You might be wrong, but just think if you're right.

Lesson 7, Heart Advice from
Gladie Burger

Bruno opened the stateroom door for me, and I walked in. Spencer's head was in an ice bucket, and he was moaning. I went to him and rubbed his back.

"I hate honeymoons, Pinky," he moaned. "I thought I would love them, but they suck balls. No, sucking balls would have been good. Honeymoons are bleeding hemorrhoids. Honeymoons are infected ingrown hairs. Honeymoons are the worst."

"It's a good sign that he's talking," Bruno announced. "Half this floor is totally laid out."

"Do you want some ginger ale?" I asked Spencer, softly.

"Don't talk about food. Please, Pinky," he said with his head in the bucket.

"I'll get the doctor to give you more morphine."

"No, way. I dreamed that snakes were crawling over my body. And in my body. From now on, it's Just Say No for me, Pinky. Ohhh…"

I put a cold compress on the back of his neck, but it wasn't helping. Spencer had it bad. I made a prayer that we would quickly make our way out of the bomb cyclone.

"How's the investigation going?" Bruno asked.

"What investigation?" Spencer moaned. "Oh, no! Here it comes."

He dropped to the floor and crawled as fast as he could to the bathroom, where he closed himself off. The sound of running water and retching followed. Then, as if the ship was sympathetic to Spencer's suffering, it began to make a terrifying creaking noise.

"It sounds like the ship is going to break apart," I said to Bruno. The sounds of the bomb cyclone competed with the ship. Wind and waves crashed against the boat, making it complain loudly. Spencer's sounds from the bathroom were completely drowned out. "It's Armageddon."

"This is good," Bruno yelled to be heard. "It means we're approaching the end of it. It's darkest before the dawn, you know."

I nodded and didn't know whether to believe him about being at the end of the horrible weather conditions. The ship was pitching and rolling worse than ever, and the noises sounded like the end of the world, not the end of the storm.

I stood with my feet wide apart to keep my balance. Bruno didn't have a problem. He stepped closer to me and inspected my face, like he was searching it for information. "So, I've seen how you've been investigating the chef's murder. What have you discovered? Maybe it's not good to rock the boat."

"The boat's already rocking," I said.

"You shouldn't ask so many questions. Do you hear me? I'm telling you to mind your own business."

I tried to take a step back, but there was nowhere to go. My back was literally against the wall. Bruno took another step toward me. He was definitely invading my personal space.

"So, what have you found out? Just between you and me. I mean, I don't want you to go around telling other people about it," he said.

Danger, Will Robinson. Suddenly, a vision of being chased and attacked flashed through my mind. My life was in danger.

"So?" Bruno continued. "You're not going to tell, are you? Just to me. What have you found out?"

"Spencer!" I called. "Spencer!"

Nothing. The world was conspiring against me, making a horrible racket so that Spencer couldn't hear me and save me.

That was fine. I would take care of myself.

I grabbed Spencer's ice bucket. It had a good heft to it, made of metal, instead of plastic. I swung it as hard as I could against Bruno's head, and he dropped like a lead balloon onto the bed.

"I got him, Spencer!" I yelled. There was still nothing. The noise was deafening, and there was no way he would be able to hear me. I went to open the bathroom door, in order to tell Spencer that I had caught the bad guy, but before I reached that door, the door to the stateroom swung open, and Hans Weber, the muesli-eating Swiss man entered.

And he was holding a long, wide knife. The kind to chop up big fish or a side of beef. I gulped. Odds were that he hadn't made a wrong turn on his way to cutting up fish for our dinner.

"Wha... huh..." I said. I couldn't think of any other words. He probably wasn't in a talking mood.

"This is over," he growled, stumbling to the left with the rocking of the ship, blocking the path between me and the bathroom. He raised the knife over his head.

In that moment, with the ship sounding like it was going to crack in half, with the storm raging like God was supremely pissed off, and with a man aiming a large knife at my head, while my husband was obliviously throwing up in the bathroom and the steward was unconscious next to me, I wondered why this sort of thing kept happening to me.

Boy was Spencer going to be peeved when he found out that I died because of my snooping. Vomiting on our honeymoon was one thing, but getting murdered really was beyond the pale. Thoughtless.

I sighed. Wow, I was a crummy wife.

"Are you going to kill me?" I asked the Swiss man, even though I already knew the answer.

"Why couldn't you leave well enough alone?" he yelled.

I shrugged. "I've been told it's a disease, like scabies."

"I didn't want to hurt you, but you're making me."

"I know. I know. I've heard it all before."

"This is your fault."

"If I had a dime for every time it's my fault, I'd be a rich woman. Get on with it. Do what you came here to do." What was I saying? I had gotten so caught up in not wanting to hear his villain monologue that I was egging him on to kill me. I blamed my short attention span on the internet. Damned instant gratification.

Weber came at me with the knife. I was out of weapons, since the ice bucket had landed on the other side of the room and Spencer was still in the bathroom. But I figured Spencer was a better bet than retrieving the ice bucket.

So, I screamed.

And I screamed.

But Mother Nature and the old Soviet-era ship screamed louder.

Spencer didn't hear me. He didn't open the bathroom door, ready to save me.

I was on my own.

I thought quickly. The room was tiny, and there was no way around him and his giant knife. No matter what acrobatic moves I could think up, he would have stabbed me at least five times before I made it to the door.

And I didn't know how to do any acrobatic moves.

I screamed again, but nobody was coming to my rescue.

The boat pitched, and my attacker stumbled to the right, blocking even more of my path to the bathroom. So, I had no choice. I took that as my cue. I jumped onto the bed, scrambling over Bruno's unconscious body, and hightailed it out of the stateroom. The bomb cyclone that had allowed me to escape was now preventing me from running for my life. As I tried to make it down the hallway, the ship rocked violently, throwing me against the walls. I fell down a million times before I got to the elevator. Weber was having an easier time, catching up to me with the knife still firmly in his hand.

Damned killers. Why were they always in better shape than I

was?

Maybe I should start eating muesli, I thought, as I pushed the elevator button repeatedly in a panic. The elevator door stayed closed. The knife was coming closer. I thought quickly and did something I almost never did.

I took the stairs.

Opening the door to the stairwell, I grabbed onto the banister with both hands. As I climbed the stairs, I was tossed around and fell to my knees at least a dozen times. Behind me, the stairwell door opened and closed. Turning around for a second, I saw the killer climbing the stairs after me. But since he was holding a knife with one hand, he only had one to hold onto the banister. Halfway up the first flight, he went over the side.

"Thank you, bomb cyclone," I said.

Two more stories, and I looked down, again. Hans Weber had gotten back over the banister and was steadily making his way up to me.

Damned muesli.

I ducked through a door to the dining room and pushed a chair against the door. "Help!" I shouted. "Killer! Knife! Muesli! Help!"

The dining room was empty. It looked like a hurricane had hit it, and I supposed it sort of had. Assorted furniture was strewn around the room. Even though it was daytime, it was only darkness through the windows.

"Help! Spencer is too young to be a widower!" I shouted, again and ran through the dining room. Actually, it was run, fall, run, fall, fall, fall through the dining room. Finally, I made it to the kitchen. "Help!"

The kitchen was empty, too. I ducked into the pantry and closed myself in. As hiding places went, it wasn't the smartest, but at least it was a hiding place. I stuffed myself behind a few crates of food and hoped for the best.

It took Hans Weber less than a minute to find me. "Stop running from me!" he yelled, out of breath and bleeding on his left temple.

"Stop trying to kill me!"

"I have to!"

I rolled my eyes. "You have to kill me? You have to kill me?" I dumped a tower of crates on him and ran for it. If I had been smarter, I would have grabbed a knife or a frying pan on my way out of the kitchen, but it was all I could do to keep one foot in front of the other.

Somehow, I managed to get on deck. There were people there, half of the psychedelics, walking around, following invisible people or whatever invisible thing they were following.

"Help!" I shouted. "Help! Killer!" I grabbed a man by his shoulders and gave him a shake. "Wake up! I need help!"

"You have a face on your face," he said and clipped some kind of red flashlight to my shirt.

"Thank you," I said. "Can you help me? A killer is after me."

"And the face on your face has three noses. The other face doesn't have any noses."

And then he was gone, walking away to find more faces, and Hans Weber was there, still with the knife in his hand. I backed up, and he stepped forward. The storm waged around us, tossing the ship like it was a toy. If we were at the edge of the storm, as Bruno said, it was a hell of an edge. The deck was slippery and ankle-deep with water. I was sure that I was going to be washed overboard and drowned, which was a relief since I had thought I was going to be stabbed to death.

"Don't do this! Don't do this!" I pleaded, as I backed up.

"I just want to have my muesli in the morning. Is that so much to ask?" he said.

I stopped in my tracks. "Huh?"

"But no! It's gourmet this and gourmet that. Heavy, heavy food morning, noon, and night. I'm living off of antacids, and every night I'm terrorized by food-induced nightmares. Do you know what that's like?"

"I live in a house with a lot of fried chicken."

"I don't care about your fried chicken!" he yelled, waving the knife at me. "I had the best life. A perfect life. Muesli at seven. Chicken and potatoes at twelve-thirty. Ham and salad at eight. Now my life is ruined!"

"It's not my fault! I didn't mean to ruin your life."

"Not you. Not you. My brother. The great chef, Fritz Weber!"

I was getting closer to understanding his craziness, but I wasn't quite there. I backed up more until my legs pressed against the railing. The psychedelics had disappeared on the other side of the deck. The weather was so bad, and it was so dark that I couldn't see beyond the back of my soon-to-be-killer.

"All was well until Fritz was terminated," Hans continued. He had crazy eyes, big and circling round and round. I had seen more than my share of crazy eyes in the past year. Murder always came with crazy eyes.

"That was very sad for him," I said. "He worked here for twenty years, and then they just up and fired him. I know what that's like. You wouldn't know it to look at me, but I've been fired a lot in my life. A lot. More than ten times. Actually, more than fifty times. Okay, okay, I'll tell you the truth. More than two hundred times."

"What are you talking about?"

"Fine! I've been fired more than two hundred times. Happy?"

"I don't care how many times you were fired!" he yelled, his voice rising over the sounds of the storm and the ship. "I don't care

elise sax

that my brother was fired. Don't you see? Don't you see?"

I didn't see. Whatever gift I had had gone dark. "Revenge?" I asked. "You wanted revenge for your brother, so you killed his replacement. Killed him with a shrimp fork as an homage to gourmet cooking?"

He lowered his hand that was holding the knife. "Are you stupid or something?"

"Not stupid… exactly."

"I didn't want revenge. I wanted my brother to get his job back."

Talk about taking brotherly love to extremes. "I understand. You loved your brother. You wanted to help him."

He took two steps forward. "Are you playing with me? Are you so stupid?"

Ding. Ding. Ding. It all came to me as an answer. "No! I understand now!" I announced. "I know exactly what happened and why."

"Pinky! Pinky! Where are you? Pinky!" Spencer's booming voice came closer, and I was filled with relief and a big chunk of euphoria.

"Over here! He's going to kill me!"

"Shut up! Shut up!" Hans screeched. "Don't move!"

He came at me with the knife. "Don't move? Who's stupid now?" I asked and lunged to the side, but I slipped in the water and went down. "Spencer! Over here! Help!"

Through the storm, I finally saw Spencer. My husband. The beautiful, muscle-bound man, who looked like he had vengeance on his mind. And also, nausea. He had lots of nausea.

"I see you! I'm coming, Pinky! Leave her alone, you bastard!"

"Over here!" another voice cried. "The faces! The faces!"

"Uh oh," I mumbled.

A group of psychedelics approached Spencer.

"Get away from me!" he yelled.

"But your face!" one of them yelled back.

"Help!" I shouted, to get the focus back on my imminent murder.

"Shut up!" Hans yelled. "Hold still!"

The psychedelics ran toward Spencer, knocking him down, while I rolled away from Hans's reach. "Help!"

"Oomph!" Spencer yelled. "Get away! That's not my face, you morons! That's not anywhere near my face!"

"Here's a face!" I called to the psychedelics. "Lots of faces on one short man! Come and get it!"

It was a longshot. The mushroom-eaters weren't exactly malleable. But it worked. With the promise of multiple faces, they moved on from Spencer like zombies with the promise of fresh brains. I rolled away, finding Spencer, as they surrounded Hans. His knife dropped to the ground.

"Faces!" I heard through the group of psychedelics, and then they held up Hans and walked him away into the ship, like he was a Superbowl MVP.

Spencer cupped my face in his hands. "Are you all right, Pinky?"

"Yes."

"I came out of the bathroom, and you were gone. Bruno was unconscious. I put two and two together and figured you were pulling another Gladie."

"Pulling another Gladie? What does that mean?" I put my hand out, palm forward, "No. Forget it. Don't tell me. How do you feel?"

"I feel confused. Confused and nauseated. I think I threw up a lung. And a good chunk of my small intestine. Rub my head, Pinky."

I rubbed his head. "Don't be confused. It's an easy story. You see, this is what happened... wait a second." I looked around. Something was happening. Something big. We had reached the end of the bomb cyclone. The sky cleared, and we were bathed in bright light. Like a miracle, the noise subsided, and the ship stopped rocking and rolling. "Peace," I said, relieved.

Spencer's green face turned back to his normal color. He stood and helped me up. "Pinky, it stopped. No more vomiting. I feel human, again. Stay here."

He left and came back a few minutes later after wrestling the killer from the psychedelics. He handed him over to the captain to lock up until the Long Beach police could get at him. When he returned, Spencer wrapped me in his arms.

"One thing's for certain," he said. "I'll never have a dull moment, married to you. So, tell me why the muesli guy killed the chef."

"Well…" I started, stepping back from him, ready to do my Miss Marple whodunit shtick. But like a hiccough after a big meal, the ship pitched violently one last time. It was an echo of the bomb cyclone. A dying gasp.

It was strong enough to knock Spencer and me off balance. As I tried not to fall, I knocked hard into Spencer. He stumbled, and unfortunately, his foot landed on Hans's knife. Since the deck was still flooded with water, the knife acted like an ice skate. I watched helplessly, as Spencer rode the knife on one foot straight for the ship's railing.

What happened next might not have happened if Spencer hadn't been weakened from two days of illness. It also might not have happened if the Russian oligarch who had renovated the old ship had decided to replace the ancient railings along with the bathroom fixtures.

Whatever it was, when Spencer hit the railing, it crumbled, and he fell right through it and down, down, down to the ocean below along with the metal pieces of the railing.

"Spencer!" I screamed. I ran to the edge of the ship and looked down. Spencer was bobbing in the water. "Climb up! Climb up!" I shouted down at him.

"Are you kidding me?" he called back.

He had a point. The ship was sailing away, and he was helpless in the water. "I'll save you!"

I jumped.

There's not a lot of logic in love. People do crazy things for the people they love. Stupid things.

So, I didn't think much before I jumped. All I knew was that the man I loved was in danger and needed help. Why I thought I could help him was beyond me.

In any case, if I didn't think much before I jumped, I thought a whole hell of a lot of things while I jumped. First, I thought: Why am I doing this? A quick second thought was: I'm afraid of heights. And third was: I'm going to get eaten by sharks. I'm going to drown. I'm going to die from the fall. I could really go for a sandwich.

And then I stopped thinking because I hit the water hard. Down I went, and I fought against my descent with everything I had. Finally, I managed to reach the top and drew breath. "Spencer!" I called.

"Pinky, what did you do?" He swam toward me.

"Are you okay?"

"Me? How about you? Are you okay?"

"I'm saving you."

"Oh, phew. I feel so much better now," he said, treading water.

"Did you just roll your eyes at me? I don't appreciate your attitude."

"Okay, truce. Did you shout 'man overboard' before you jumped, by any chance?"

We watched the cruise ship sail away. "I don't remember."

"I'll take that as a no."

"It's not my fault."

"I know."

"I was worried about you."

"I know."

"I didn't want you to die."

"I know."

"I didn't want you to drown or get eaten by a shark."

"I know."

"I was being a good wife. Good wives jump in after their husbands when they fall overboard. It's a thing. I read it in a magazine." We were quiet for a moment. "Are you mad at me? Did you stop talking to me?"

"I'm looking around for debris that we can hang onto. We might be here for the long haul, and we'll need some relief from treading water."

There was ocean as far as the eye could see. For the first time, the enormity of our situation hit me.

We were going to die.

"We're going to die," I said.

"No, we're not," Spencer insisted. "I'm going to find some floating debris, and when a boat passes by, we'll scream, and they'll pick us up."

"Sunset is in a couple hours. And the ocean is big, Spencer. They'll never find us."

"Yes, they will."

"No, they won't."

"There! I see something floating. Hang onto me, Pinky, so we don't get separated. I'm going to swim us to it. We're going to be fine."

I held on to the back of his shoulders, and he swam to whatever was floating. "I should have shouted overboard," I whined. "I should have thrown in a life vest or something. We're going to die."

"We're not going to die."

"And it's going to get dark, and the water will be spooky. I'm going to be scared. Hey, wait a second. One of those mushroom people gave me a flashlight." I held onto Spencer's shoulder with one hand as he swam, and with the other, I inspected the gizmo that was still clipped to my shirt. It looked like a small flashlight with a red end. GPS Beacon was written on the side of it. I flipped a switch, and the light began to flash, and it made a beeping noise.

"I think I hear a ship, Pinky," Spencer announced.

"You do?"

"Yes. We're saved! We're saved!" He stopped swimming and turned around to face me. "I thought we were dead for sure, but we're saved! I really thought we were goners. Pinky, your boobs are glowing."

"That's just my GPS beacon. What do you mean, you thought we were dead for sure?"

"You had a GPS beacon all this time?"

"I thought it was a flashlight. Is a GPS beacon good?"

"Yes! It means we're saved!"

He hugged me, and we started to sink, so he let me go. "Are we really saved?" I asked.

"Yes. It might take a while, but we'll be saved. I mean it this time."

I bobbed in the water for a moment. Swimming in the middle of the ocean was scary. Who knew what was underneath me in the dark depths? Spencer sensed my fear. "Let's take our minds off this. Tell me why the Swiss guy killed the chef?" he asked.

I perked up. "His villain monologue was cut short, but I figured it out."

"Well, shoot, Miss Marple. Give me the rundown."

"Hans Weber's brother was Fritz Weber, the former chef of the cruise ship," I started, happy to tell him whodunit and why. "Fritz was fired to make way for the newest in food fads. Unfortunately for Hans, Fritz moved in with him when he was fired. Hans liked to eat simple, light food, but now he had a gourmet chef living with him, cooking up a storm. So, it's all about food."

"All about what?" Spencer asked.

"Food. Hans wanted Fritz to get his job back so that he could get back to eating muesli. It was all about food."

"So, he killed the old chef to get rid of his brother."

"So that his brother would get his old job back."

"People are weird, Pinky."

"Tell me about it. You doing okay? You look tired," I said.

"Treading water is tiring. You don't look tired at all, though. Are you a super swimmer, and you never told me?"

"I'm not treading water," I told him. "I'm floating. You're not floating?"

"No," he said and laughed.

"What? What? Why is that funny?"

"Nothing, Pinky. Forget it."

"What's funny about me floating?"

"Muscle doesn't float," he said, still laughing.

"What?" My face grew hot. "Oh." I splashed him. "Women have higher fat percentages than men."

"Uh huh," he said, still laughing.

"I ate a salad last week!"

"I know. I know." He kept laughing.

"I thought you like my junk in the trunk."

Spencer pulled my floating body to him. "I like all your junk, Pinky. Every bit of it."

"You're going to really like it when you have to hold onto me so you don't drown."

"Oh, Pinky. I drowned the moment I saw you on the telephone pole."

It took twenty-five minutes for the Coast Guard to find us. They gave us dry clothes and took us to shore, where my emergency contact Bridget met us, along with Lucy, who hired a limo to pick us up. The cruise line was going to send us our belongings later, which was fine with me because I never wanted to go on the ship again. Neither did Spencer. In fact, for the first time, he was glad that our Jacuzzi tub was destroyed along with our custom-made house.

"Honeymoons suck," he told me on the deck of the Coast Guard ship as we reached port.

"Don't I know it," I said.

"Marriage is great, though."

"I second that."

"Let's keep doing the marriage thing, but let's pass on all future honeymoon activities."

"All honeymoon activities?"

Spencer smirked his little smirk. "The travel honeymoon

86

activities. The rest we can keep."

When we got off the boat, Lucy and Bridget ran to hug me.

"You bagged another killer?" Lucy asked. "I miss all the fun."

"He chased me with a knife while we were in a bomb cyclone," I said.

"You're amazing," Bridget said. "Susan B. Anthony, Margaret Sanger, and you."

"I fell overboard," Spencer said, but they ignored him.

"How are things in Cannes?" I asked them, as we walked to the limo. "Did I miss something?"

Bridget shot a look at Lucy, but she kept her mouth shut.

"What?" I asked. "What did I miss?"

"Well, Ruth called to tell me that Zelda and she were leaving the boat to go find some man in the wild west."

"Wild West? You mean, like Santa Monica?"

"I think she's after a cowboy," Bridget said and adjusted her glasses and looked away.

"Wait a minute. What's going on?" I asked. "Did I miss something else?"

Lucy stopped walking and raised her hands high. "Triplets!"

she shouted. "I'm having triplets. We just found out. I'm going to be as big as a house. Do you know how much plastic surgery I'm going to need after triplets?"

I hugged her. "Congratulations!"

She pushed me away. "Do not congratulate me, darlin'. Harry had to call the doctor when he heard."

"Why? Are you all right?"

"Yes, but he isn't. He's in bed, sedated. I don't know how they're going to keep him sedated for the next eighteen years, though. And what am I going to do? You know I don't believe in plastic surgery. How will I get my figure back?"

"You don't believe in plastic surgery?" Bridget asked, arching an eyebrow. Lucy gave her a death stare. "Okay. You don't believe in plastic surgery."

I put my arm around Lucy's shoulders. "It's going to be great, Lucy. Three times the fun. Maybe they'll be friends like the three of us."

Lucy seemed to think of that for a moment. "That sounds pretty good. Friends like the three of us. Happy and loved forever. That's almost worth the stretch marks. What am I talking about? Nothing's worth stretch marks!"

Read *Die Noon*, the first in the *Goodnight Mysteries*. Follow

Matilda Dare in her hilarious adventures as she solves mysteries and falls in love.

And don't forget to sign up for the newsletter for new releases and special deals: http://www.elisesax.com/mailing-list.php

ABOUT THE AUTHOR

Elise Sax writes hilarious happy endings. She worked as a journalist, mostly in Paris, France for many years but always wanted to write fiction. Finally, she decided to go for her dream and write a novel. She was thrilled when *An Affair to Dismember*, the first in the *Matchmaker Mysteries* series, was sold at auction.

Elise is an overwhelmed single mother of two boys in Southern California. She's an avid traveler, a swing dancer, an occasional piano player, and an online shopping junkie.

Friend her on Facebook: facebook.com/ei.sax.9
Send her an email: elisesax@gmail.com
You can also visit her website: elisesax.com
And sign up for her newsletter to know about new releases and sales: elisesax.com/mailing-list.php
Or tweet at her: @theelisesax

Made in the USA
Middletown, DE
16 February 2021